EGYPTIAN TALES

THE PHANTOM OF THE NILE

Bloomsbury Education
An imprint of Bloomsbury Publishing Plc

50 Bedford Square
London
WC1B 3DP
UK

1385 Broadway
New York
NY 10018
USA

www.bloomsbury.com

BLOOMSBURY and the Diana logo are trademarks of Bloomsbury Publishing Plc

First published in Great Britain 2011
This paperback edition published in 2017

A catalogue record for this book is available from the British Library.

ISBN
PB: 978 1 4729 4217 3
epub: 978 1 4729 5255 4
epdf: 978 1 4729 5254 7

2 4 6 8 10 9 7 5 3 1

Typeset by Newgen Knowledge Works (P) Ltd., Chennai, India

Printed and bound in UK by CPI Group (UK) ltd, Croydon CR0 4YY

TERRY DEARY

EGYPTIAN TALES

THE PHANTOM OF THE NILE

Illustrated by Helen Flook

BLOOMSBURY EDUCATION
AN IMPRINT OF BLOOMSBURY
LONDON OXFORD NEW YORK NEW DELHI SYDNEY

CHAPTER 1
The Miserable Master

"Do you believe in ghosts?" Menes whispered to his friend Ahmose.

Menes heard the sudden swish of a stick and then felt it strike him on the back.

"No talking in class!" the fat and sweating teacher hissed.

"Sorry, Master Meshwesh," Menes muttered. He bent his head over the plaster board in front of him. He dipped his reed pen in water, rubbed it against the black ink-block and started writing again.

Lessons were in a cool garden with a sparkling fountain. But still Menes sweated over his work.

But fat Master Meshwesh wasn't finished with him yet.

"You will never be a good scribe if you talk when you should be working, will you, Menes?"

"No, Master Meshwesh," the boy sighed.

"But, if you work hard, you will grow to be a temple scribe and as rich as a lord. You'd like that, wouldn't you, Menes?"

"Yes, Master Meshwesh."

The teacher was panting in the midday sun and licking his thick lips.

"Yes, Master Meshwesh,"
he mimicked.

"Rich. Learn to write and you can become a priest. Or even a corn dealer, like Ahmose's father. Not like your father. A poor and stinking fisherman. If you talk in class I'll have you thrown out of school and you'll end up like your fishy, foul father."

Suddenly the master grabbed Menes by the ear and lifted the boy to his feet. He breathed his onion breath into the boy's face. "Have you brought any fish from home for me?"

“Yes, Master Meshwesh!” Menes squealed as the fat thumb and finger squeezed his ear.

“Good,” the teacher said. “In that case we will stop for lunch.”

The ten boys rinsed their pens in the water, stood up and stretched. Menes opened his linen bag and took out two pieces of dried fish and some bread. The teacher let loose the boy’s ear, snatched the food in one huge paw and grinned his gap-toothed grin.

"Tasty!" he said and smacked his lips.

"One fish was for me," Menes said.

"Well, I've just taken it from you as a punishment," Master Meshwesh said. He walked over to the shade of a garden wall and began to fill his face with the food in one hand and then wash it down with a flask of beer in the other.

The boys knew he would sleep for an hour after lunch as he did every day. They would be free to talk.

Menes shook his head. "Tell me, Ahmose, do you think learning to write will make us rich?"

Ahmose was the same age as Menes but his father was a wealthy corn dealer. "If we can write, the temple will pay us well to work. Maybe one of the lords will give us a job. Yes, being a scribe will make us rich."

"So why is Master Meshwesh a teacher? Why isn't he making money at the temple?" Menes asked.

Ahmose took his friend by the arm and dragged him around the corner of the garden wall so they were hidden from the bullying master.

He spoke quickly and quietly. "He was the scribe to Payneshi, the governor of our region. He had to keep a record of all the corn and the animals, the gold and the jewels, the slaves and the wine of Payneshi."

"An important job," Menes said.

"But Master Meshwesh used his scribe skills to cheat Payneshi. If Payneshi got two bags of gold then Meshwesh wrote that he had *one* bag of gold, you see?"

Menes shook his head. "No."

"Meshwesh wrote one bag of gold on the list – and there was one bag of gold in Payneshi's counting house. The other bag of gold would go into Meshwesh's pocket, you see?"

"Did he have big pockets?" Menes asked.

Ahmose groaned. "I don't mean he put it in his pocket – I mean he pinched it. He was caught when the pharaoh sent a box of jewels to Payneshi and then sent a message to ask if Payneshi liked them."

"Did he?" Menes asked.

"He never got them! Payneshi realised Meshwesh must have stolen them," Ahmose explained. "He was furious."

"Did he get the box of jewels back?" Menes asked.

"No. Meshwesh must have hidden them. He said he knew nothing about them. Payneshi banished Meshwesh from the city of Karnak for five years. Now he's back to torment us. No one trusts him – no one will give him a scribe job – so he has to be a teacher," Ahmose said. "See?"

Menes shook his head. "No."

"No?"

"If he really did hide the treasure then he'd just go and find it."

"Maybe he forgot where it was," Ahmose said.

"Would you forget where you'd hidden

a fortune?" Menes asked.

Ahmose shook his head. "It's a mystery... and talking about mysteries why did you ask if I believed in ghosts?"

"Because there's a foul phantom in the new house at the temple gate," Menes said. "Old Maiarch is being driven from her home. I have to use my scribe skills. And I have to kill it!"

CHAPTER 2
The Fearful Phantom

Ahmose shuddered even though the noon-day sun was scorching the street.

"How do you know the phantom won't kill *you*?" he asked.

Menes shrugged. "It's a chance I have to take." He peered around the corner of the wall. Master Meshwesh was dozing in the shade. "Come with me."

"Are we going to see the ghost?"

"We are going to see old Maiarch," Menes

said as he led the way down the cool alleys that led to the Temple of Horus.

"Is she dead?"

"No, but she nearly died of fright when she saw the phantom," Menes said. "She woke up in the middle of a moonless night and saw him. Just a shape in the

starlight. He was big as an ox. He roared like a hippo when she woke up."

"You can't kill a phantom – not a

monster like that," Ahmose said. "You're a scribe, not a soldier."

Menes laughed. "And it's my reed pen I'm going to use to kill him," he said.

"You can't stab a phantom with a reed pen," Ahmose argued.

Menes hurried on. "When the king dies they wrap him as a mummy. And inside the wrapping they put the Book of the Dead. The book is full of prayers that will help the spirit in the Afterlife. Protect it from the monsters that are

waiting there to attack it. We all need a Book of the Dead – even if we aren't rich enough to be made into mummies."

Ahmose nodded. "I've heard about the monsters. There's a snake that spits poison at you."

"And boiling hot lakes," Menes reminded him.

"Rivers of fire."

"And at the end of it all there's the Devourer waiting for you. Part crocodile, part hippo and part lion. If you've been evil he rips out your heart and eats it!" Menes cried.

"That's why people need us so much. We can write the prayers that will help them."

Ahmose smiled. "I see. You have written prayers for Maiarch to drive away the phantom."

"I have," Menes said. "She promised to pay me well. Maybe enough to buy my dad a new boat. Without a boat he can't fish. Without fish to sell my family will starve."

"I could lend you money," Ahmose said.

Menes gripped his arm. "Thanks, friend. But it would be better if I could earn it myself. Maybe she'll pay me today."

They turned a corner into the great paved square in front of the temple.

"This is Maiarch's house," Menes said, leading the way through an arch into a fine garden. There was a large pond with golden fish swimming in sparkling water. Trees gave shade and flowers covered the grass. "Maiarch is very rich," Menes explained. "She had this new house built just for herself."

"It's even bigger than our house," Ahmose said.

The boys walked into the shadowy darkness of the house. An ancient woman lay on a low couch. Her skin was wrinkled and pale as old parchment. Her eyes were bright as a bird's.

"Good day, Maiarch," Menes said. "This is my friend Ahmose."

"Sit down, sit down," the old woman croaked. The boys sat on the floor.

"Did it work?" Menes asked.

"Did it work? he says. Did it work? It did not. Hopeless. Useless. Worthless scrap of parchment."

"The phantom came back?"

"The phantom came back? he says. Came back? He came back twice as large, twice as ugly and twice as evil. He says that if I'm still here when he comes back tonight he'll crush me like a scarab beetle. And he could too. He's big enough to crush a crocodile."

The old woman spread her arms wide to show how big the phantom was. Suddenly she swept her arms forward and pointed at Menes. "So you needn't think I am paying you anything, young scribe. You're hopeless, useless, worthless."

CHAPTER 3
The Greedy Ghost

Menes sniffed away a tear. "I'll try again," he offered.

"He'll try again!" Maiarch cackled."Well

you won't try your silly prayers. They're hopeless, useless, worthless."

"Maybe we could try something else," Ahmose put in.

"Someone will have to do something," the old woman moaned. "The gods will be very angry."

"Uh? Why?" Ahmose asked.

"Why? he says. Why? Because the phantom didn't just disturb my sleep and threaten me. He walked up to my altar... see it there?"

The boys looked at the wall behind them. A lamp lit the stone statue of the god Bes – an ugly dwarf.

"Bes looks after women and children," Menes said.

"He's supposed to – my old legs won't get me to the temple, so I have my own altar in the house. Every day I put fish, bread and beer on the altar for Bes."

"Does he eat it?" Menes asked. He'd always wanted to know what happened to the food offered to the gods in the temple. They seemed to eat a lot.

"He doesn't usually eat it," Maiarch said. "But last night he didn't even have the chance. When the phantom had finished frightening me he walked up to the altar and pinched all the fish and bread and beer. The cheek of it. He packed it in his mouth and said he'd be back tonight."

"That's no phantom," Ahmose said. "Phantoms don't eat fish. They eat human spirits. I don't think you have a ghost, old lady."

"Here! Here! Here! Watch who you're calling old," Maiarch squawked. "I'm only sixty summers old – King Pepi lived to a hundred or more."

Ahmose sighed. "What I'm saying is you have a common thief. He's just trying to scare you so he can rob you."

Menes shook his head. "But why doesn't he just take what he wants? Old Maiarch can't stop him."

"Now *you're* calling me old, you young monkey," Maiarch moaned.

Ahmose nodded slowly. "So, what does he want?"

"The best way to find out is to ask him," Menes said.

Ahmose's mouth fell open. "You think a thief will stop and chat?"

"He will if we've captured him. If we make him talk," Menes said. "We'll be here tonight. We'll grab him and force him to talk."

"He's stronger than an ox," Ahmose reminded him.

"Big enough to crush a crocodile," Maiarch added.

"Don't worry," Menes told them.

"I have a fool-proof plan."

"Better than your hopeless, useless, worthless scrap of parchment?" the old woman asked.

"Much better."

"What's the plan?" Ahmose asked.

"I'll tell you after school," Menes promised.

CHAPTER 4
Opet and Beer

At the end of the afternoon Menes raced through the city, over the fields and down to the small house of baked mud at the edge of the Nile.

His father was trying to patch his old boat with reeds while his younger sisters worked on mending the nets.

His mother was pouring beer from a large stone jar – straining it through a linen cloth into a bowl. "What's wrong with your back?" she asked when she saw her son's red and purple marks.

He shrugged. "Master Meshwesh beat me for talking."

"I know teachers are told to beat bad boys," she sighed, "but Meshwesh seems to enjoy it. Let me get you some beer and bread for dinner."

"I'll have this," Menes said, reaching for the bowl.

"No you won't!" his father cried. "That is extra strong beer. It's for the Festival of Opet tonight. I've been waiting for weeks to taste that beer. That would knock out an ox, that beer!"

"Would it?" Menes murmured. He took the jug of weak beer and swallowed hungrily.

His mother smiled. "You are a growing boy. You enjoy your food. I wish we had more."

He would have had more if Meshwesh hadn't stolen his lunch.

"Sorry, no fresh fish today," his father said. "I'd be crocodile-food if I tried to go out in this," he added and gave the old boat a kick.

"Never mind," Menes' mother told his father. "Tonight you can join the Festival of Opet. Forget your cares for a while. Are you coming to the temple with us, Menes?"

The boy licked the last crumb from his fingers and said, "No. I am going to make us rich tonight. I'm going to buy Father a new boat."

His mother laughed. "You're a good boy. That would be nice." But he could tell she didn't believe him.

As darkness fell his father and mother went into the house to put on their ragged clothes, but the best they had. Menes poured the strong beer into a flask and replaced it with weak beer. "Sorry, Father," he whispered.

His parents left as the star Sirius rose in the sky. "The goddess Isis is looking down on us. Time to go," his father said.

When he was sure his sisters were playing happily in the house, Menes gathered up his father's net and his writing tools and followed his parents down the dark road to the city. It was time to meet and defeat the phantom.

CHAPTER 5
The Fallen Phantom

The square in front of the temple was crowded with people. The noise would wake a mummy in its tomb. The priests of the temple of Karnak carried a statue of the god Amun into the square where it

met another group of priests carrying the statue of the goddess Mut.

The people cheered when the two statues met and the drinking began. Menes pushed his way through to the gateway of Maiarch's house. In the shadows he saw Ahmose waiting for him.

"Is Maiarch safely out of the way?" Menes asked.

"My father has offered her a bed at our house for the Opet Festival," he said. "She grumbled, but she went. Our servants carried her."

"On with the plan, then," Menes said. "Get onto the couch, wear the old woman's wig and I'll hide in that chest."

The boys hurried to set up their trap and then they waited.

The only light was the lamp by the statue of the god Bes. His ugly face glowed and watched as Menes placed the large bowl of strong beer in front of him. "Sorry, Bes, but it's not for you!"

Ahmose lay on the couch while Menes climbed into the chest and held his reed pen and a piece of parchment. "I'll make a note of everything he says. Then we'll go to the governor and have him arrested."

The noise of the crowd outside roared and swirled around them. So they didn't

hear the phantom when he arrived. "Still here, old woman?" the voice roared.

Ahmose jumped.

Menes peered out from the lid of the chest and made out the figure of a large

man with a black cloth over his head to hide his face. There were holes cut out for his mouth and eyes.

Ahmose called back, "Here! Here!

Here! Watch who you're calling old. I'm only sixty summers old – King Pepi lived to a hundred or more."

"You're old enough to be my granny," the phantom snarled.

"No I'm not, you young monkey!" Ahmose said and his voice was perfect.

"Look, you withered old baboon, if I can't scare you out then I'll have to throw you out," he said and moved towards the couch.

"Phantoms can't hurt the living," Ahmose told him.

"No?"

"No! You're just a spirit. You can't pick me up."

"Yes I can! I'm an extra-strong spirit."

"Prove it."

"How?"

"Let me see... pick up that bowl of beer by the statue of Bes," Ahmose said and waved a shaking finger towards the statue by the lamp.

The phantom wandered across to the table and picked up the bowl of strong beer. "See? Told you!" he crowed.

"But I'll bet you can't drink it," Ahmose urged.

"Watch me," the phantom said and sipped the beer.

"Ooooh! Nice drop of beer that," he said smacking his lips. "I've had

a few tonight but none as nice and strong as this." He put it to his lips and swallowed it all.

Then he stepped back. He seemed to catch his heel on the rush mat and sat down heavily. "Oooof!" he grunted and then belched. He swayed. "Ooooh! Just have a little sit down, I think."

The big body swayed and the mask hung crookedly so he was looking out through one eye and the mouth-hole.

"Just sit down? You didn't come here to sit down. You came to rob me, you villain!" Ahmose cried.

"Rob 'oo," the phantom said. "Not rob 'oo. Just come to get what belongs to me."

Menes slowly raised the lid of the chest further. He put down the pen and picked up the net.

The phantom didn't seem to notice. He was too busy trying to talk to Ahmose on the old woman's couch. And talking was hard because the words were getting muddled in his mouth.

"What belongs to you, you villain?" Ahmose asked as Menes crept around behind him.

"Me tresher... me trea-sure. I buried it here five summers ago before I was banished from Karnak. I hid it under the floor of me house. But when I came back I found you'd knocked down me house and built yours in its place."

Suddenly the large man began to sob. "Me tresher! Me lovely tresher. All I want's me treeeesher! Waaaagggghhhh!"

And to soak up the tears he pulled off the mask.

Ahmose jumped from the bed as Menes jumped from the shadows to throw the net over the fat man. "Master Meshwesh!" the boys cried.

"Wesh mesh?" the man babbled. "Wish-wash, mess-mish!"

As Menes tied the rope tightly the fat teacher rolled onto the floor and began to snore.

CHAPTER 6
The Terrible Teacher

The governor's guards came and took the terrible teacher away. That night they dug up the treasure and returned it to their master, Payneshi.

The next day Meshwesh was dragged in front of the Governor. "I should have you beaten to death, Meshwesh," he said.

"Yes, governor," Meshwesh groaned.

"And I should give the beating job to the young scribes." The whole school was there to see the trial. "Would you like that boys?" Payneshi asked.

"Yes!" the boys roared.

"But really it is for Menes and Ahmose to decide. You are theirs to deal with as they please. If they want you chopped into fifty pieces and thrown to the crocodiles then that is what I will order."

The fat teacher looked at the boys, his red eyes puffed and pitiful. "It would hurt."

Menes looked at Ahmose and then up at Payneshi the judge. "Spare him," Menes said quietly. "He's really taught us a lot –

he's a very good scribe but not a very good man – and he's been punished. He's lost his treasure."

Payneshi blinked. "It's *my* treasure."

"Sorry," Menes said quickly. "Spare him. Let him go back to teaching us... but take his beating sticks away."

Payneshi said, "A wise young man and a generous one."

"Very generous," Meshwesh whined.

"But I can be generous too," Payneshi said. "I am giving you half of all the treasure that Meshwesh stole. It is your reward."

And so Menes walked from the palace a rich young man.

"What will you buy?" his mother asked him when he reached home.

"A boat for Dad," he said.

"I should think so too," his father grumbled. "You owe it to me."

Mother threw her head back and laughed. "You stole his strong beer. He loves strong spirits. We got to the festival and he took a drink. All he tasted was weak beer. He nearly choked."

"Ah," Menes said wisely. "Just like the phantom who drank it – he thought he was a strong spirit too!"

AFTERWORD

Egyptian schools could be cruel places – it seems schoolboys could be lazy and easily bored... just like today, really! Teachers were told to beat them because the Egyptians believed beating boys was the best way to make them work.

School was worth it though, if you could learn to write and get a job as a scribe. Once a boy had learned how to write, he could have the best jobs in Egypt – in the king's palace or in the temples. While peasants sweated in the fields, the scribes had comfortable and rich lives.

YOU TRY

1. Hard hieroglyphics

Egyptian scribes learned hieroglyphics, which were more like pictures than our letters. Here is a hieroglyphic alphabet. Write a letter to a friend using it, and decode their note to you.

A H O V

B I P W

C J Q X

D K R Y

E L S Z

F M T

G N U

2. Misery Map

In the story, Menes and Ahmose talk about what may be waiting in the Afterlife. They say there will be a snake that spits poison, boiling hot lakes, and rivers of fire to brave. At the end of it all, they say, there's the Devourer waiting for you: he was part crocodile, part hippo and part lion, and would eat out your heart!

Draw a map of the journey through the Egyptian underworld, with pictures of all the horrors you would face. Why not add a few new terrors of your own?

Terry Deary Saxon Tales

Find more fantastically fun (and sometimes gory) adventures in Terry Deary's *Saxon Tales*. Based on real historical events!